For Julie Watts, with gratitude—M.W.

*For Marina Messiha and Adelaide Carmody Stolbe,
for their inspired contributions—A.S.*

First published by Penguin Group (Australia),
a division of Pearson Australia Group Pty Ltd., 2006

Anne Spudvilas completed the illustrations for this book with
the assistance of the Eleanor Dark Foundation through
a fellowship at Varuna Writers' Retreat and Literary Centre.

Printed in China
Designed by Helen Robinson
First U.S. edition, 2007

Library of Congress Cataloging-in-Publication Data

Wild, Margaret.
Woolvs in the sitee / Margaret Wild ; Anne Spudvilas. — 1st U.S. ed.
p. cm.
Summary: In a mostly abandoned city, Ben lives in a musty
basement room, terrified of the "woolvs" that dwell in the shadows
outside, with only an upstairs neighbor, Mrs. Radinski, to help him
cope with his fears.
ISBN 978-1-59078-500-3 (hardcover : alk. paper)
[1. Fear—Fiction. 2. City and town life—Fiction. 3. Orphans—Fiction.
4. Horror stories—Fiction.] I. Spudvilas, Anne, ill. II. Title. III. Title:
Wolves in the city.
PZ7.W64574Woo 2007
[Fic]—dc22
2006039098

FRONT STREET
An Imprint of Boyds Mills Press, Inc.
815 Church Street
Honesdale, Pennsylvania 18431

WOOLVS IN THE SITEE

Margaret **Wild**
Anne **Spudvilas**

FRONT STREET
Asheville, North Carolina

There are WOOLVS in the sitee. Oh, yes!
In the streets, in the parks, in the allees.

In shops, in rustee playgrownds,

in howses rite next dor.

And soon they will kum.

They will kum for me and for yoo

and for yor bruthers and sisters.

yor muthers and fathers, yor arnts and unkils,

yor grandfathers and grandmuthers.

No won is spared.

Lissen to me.

LISSEN!

I yoosed to hav a familee, a home.
These streets wer my rivers,
these parks my vallees.

Now I am scrooched up in won room
in a mustee basement, hevy kertins akross
the window.

I peers **throo** the kertins.
I peers at the **stranj**, streekee
sunsets.

The sitee is **hush**, the traffik long-
ago **gon**. Ownlee now and agen do
I heer the swish of a **bisikil.**

I don't **need** to sqint owt the
window to no that the rider
is glansing over his sholder,
terrefied.

I longs for bl00 skys.
I longs for it to rane.
But the seesons are
topsee-turvee.

Nothing is rite.

Sumtimes I opens the dor a chink.
Then I creeps up the stares to ask my naybor
if she can spare sum water.

Missus Radinski's veree kind, but she
won't lissen abowt the WOOlvs.

"Yoo need to get owt more," she sez.
"Go bak to skool, take up a hobbee."

She dusn't unnerstand abowt the woolvs.
She thinks I'm torking abowt those luvlee
wyld creechis, running in the woods.
That's not wot I meens.

Not at all!

These WOOTVS are hatefuls,
and hating.
They are in the sitee,
they are evereewhere.

They spare no won.

LISSEN.
LISSEN.
MISSUS
RADINSKI!

Won day Missus Radinski dus lissen. But she sez, "Why do YOO call them woolvs, Ben? YOO no that can't be."

"Can't it?" I say. "Yoo MUST hav seen there shadows, Missus. Yoo MUST hav!"

"No," she sez. "I haven't seen anee shadows."

But I no she has. She has seen those shadows prowling along pavments, snarling up walls.

That's why she stares up at the sky wen she goes serching for water with her littil buket. She offen trips. Grazes an elbow. a nee. I don't blame her for not looking down.

Erly won morning,
wen I'm squinching owt
the window,
I sees a bloo sky!
A bloo sky with soft
wite clowds!

My hart leeps!
Things are bak to normal!

Suddenly I'm owt of my room.

owt of the bilding.
I'm running akross the street.
I'm tuching the sky, hugging the sky.

But it's **not** a reel sky. **Sumwon** has painted the wall bloo. A **hot** summer **bloo**. A bloo like all those summers **long** ago.

—

The **wall** is starting to darken. There are **shadows** all over it. Woolvish **shadows** krawling. **Krawling** toawards me. I cannot moov. I **shuts** my eyes.

Then **sumthing** grabs me.

Missus Radinski is here, barefoot,
hare unbrushed, as if she has just
lept owt of bed.

She is trembling. She holds me tite.

She pulls me bak to the bilding,
helps me up the stares.
Puts a blanket arownd me,
holds me as she wood a small child.

"It will all be fine agen, won of these days, I am shore," she sez as she creeps bak to her own room.

I now hav no more fernicha to bern.
Veree littil food, not much water.

For three days I taps on Missus Radinski's dor.
"Hello," I wispers. "It's me, Ben.
Missus Radinski!"
But she dusn't anser.

On the forth day, I noks agen.
Turns the handil.
Unlokt.

I slips into the hallway.
calling softly. "Missus,"
wonting to heer her say as yooshul,
"Ah, Ben. It is yoo."

I cheks the lownj room and the dining room.
They are immak—not a thing owt of place—
but there is a skeeting of dust on the tabil.

I runs to the bedroom, hoping she is sleeping,
perhaps ill, but nuthing. She is gon. Ownlee
her smell is still here—sunshinee, sopish.

Oh, Missus Radinski!

I thinks of her at the mersee of the woolvs.
I thinks abowt that time she ran owt to reskew me.
She was so veree afrade, but still she kame.
still she kame.

I ransaks the cubords, grabs a bag,
stuffles in warm klothing, tinned food,
matchis, a torch. Before I leeves,
I scrawls a messij in the dust.
"I've gon looking for yoo. Yor frend Ben."

Then I shiffles the bag over my sholder,
shuts the dor, and goes owt of the
bilding.

I stares at the painted wall. It is now as
dark as the sky at midnite, but underneeth
I no it is a hot summer bloo.

My hart is jakhammering, but I will no longer let the WOOLVS forse me to scrooch.

I will no longer let them stop me from making the streets my rivers and the parks my vallees.

Joyn me.